Only He Can

Motivational Poetry and Insight

Olivia Kapfunde

ISBN 979-8-88540-785-4 (paperback)
ISBN 979-8-88540-786-1 (digital)

Christian Faith Publishing
832 Park Avenue
Meadville, PA 16335
www.christianfaithpublishing.com

All scripture references are from King James Version (KJV).

Printed in the United States of America

Preface

Abba, for his promises are yes and amen. I proclaim the Abrahamic blessings shall define our existence, your existence.

Mega manifestation of his glorious grace upon our lives. All for your *glory,* Lord.

Thank you for everything that is and that is to be, Selah!

Thank you for you always correcting the things that concern me, pouring your love upon me, springing forth a new zeal, *Abba,* lover of my soul.

A wonderful year, *full of milestones* and good cheer—thanksgiving unto you, Lord Adonai, for the past, present, and future as we enter a season of *victory, joy, and laughter.*

As you sensitize me, Lord, synchronize all that you have for me and my heart's desire. Let it emerge in perfect harmony for your *glory,* Lord, as you will.

Gracious you are, Lord, as I proclaim, I decree and declare *unstoppable* momentum and redeeming time lost. Adonai, for this is who you are and that is what you do, for *it* shall be so!

All honor and *glory*, for you reign over all, Adonai. Getting ready for a bountiful week and season impacted by unprecedented favor. Let your week be highly favorable in all spheres of influence. Great are his *mighty* works.

Cherish them all with gratitude and thanksgiving always.

When the Lord has anointed you, you overcome all odds that come and rise against you.

Kingdom assignments.
Hallelujah! Amen.

Your will as you will.
My desire, my will…
Let it emerge in perfect harmony,
Synchronize my heart's desire as you will.
So, it shall be the birth of a new thing.
For your glory, for it to be so.

Psalm 21:2
Thou hast given him his heart's desire, and hast not with-
held the request of his lips.

Let it flow, flow.
In perfect harmony with you Lord.
Let it flow, let it flow.
For in thy presence I dwell.
Let it flow, let it flow.
Fountain of Living Waters, flowing from the Throne of Grace.
Flow, flow, let it flow.

John 7:37
He that believeth on me, as the scripture hath said, out of his belly shall flow
Rivers of living water.

More and more…
Do we not all yearn for it to be more?
Greater magnitude for all that is before us.
For so it shall be,
Grateful we will be.

2 Corinthians 9:8
And God is able to make all grace abound towards you that ye, always having all sufficiency in all things may abound to every good work.

Deuteronomy 30:9
And the Lord thy God will make thee plenteous in every good work of thine hand, in fruit of thy body in fruit of thy cattle, and in the fruit of thy Land for good: for the LORD will rejoice over thee for good as he rejoiced over thy fathers.

Forever loved,
Forever protected,
Forever guided,
Forever cleansed,
Forever consoled,
For you are forever faithful,
This is who you are ADONAI.

Psalm 139:17
How precious also are thy thoughts unto me, O God! How
great is the sum of them!

Seated upon the throne,
He reigns, he reigns.
In the upper earth and beyond,
Roundabout…
He reigns, he reigns.
Crowned in glory,
Can you not see it…?
Can you not perceive it…?
He is, the Lord of lords.

Psalm 111:6
He has shown his people the power of his works; that he may give them the
heritage of the heathen.

As I dwell in the glory of his grace,
Oh, yes I am.
A divine shift emerges…
Steadfast I am, holding onto his promise,
He fails me not.
For I was called in weakness and gathered in greatness,
So true it is.
Glory and strength abound unto me.

John 1:16
And of his fullness have all we received and grace for grace.

Corinthians 12:9
My Grace towards you is such that my Glory will shine through you and my power be seen upon you.

Our plea unto him…
To the next level Lord,
Oh yes, the next Level…
Give us the Grace to do the right thing by you as you
will Lord, Grace to do that is pleasing in thy sight.
Thank you for everything…
That's becoming and that's to be.

Psalm 24:7–8
*Lift your heads, oh ye gates and be lifted up, ye everlasting
doors and the King of glory shall come in.*
*Who is the King of glory? The Lord, strong and mighty in
battle.*

Abba! Abba! Abba!
The King of kings,
You're King.
Crowned in Glory,
He's seated on the throne,
Let him reign, Let him reign.

Revelation 4:11
Thou art worthy, O Lord, to receive glory and honor and power, for thou hast created all things, and for thy pleasure they are and were created.

He heals, He Heals.
Spiritual healing,
Physical healing,
Emotional healing.
Come drink from the well that never runs dry,
Jesus the well that never runs dry.

3 John 1:2
Beloved, I wish above all things that though mayest proper
and be in health
even as thy soul prospers.

Adonai!
In whom I trust.
Resting in you Lord,
I pour out my burdens.
"He answers!"
My Yoke is broken.
You're not a man that you should lie Lord,
For I am now free.

Psalm 16:11
Thou wilt shew me thy path of life: in thy presence is fullness
of joy; at thy right hand there are pleasures for evermore.

Arise! Arise!
It might be uncertain,
A leap of faith shall set you in motion.
Yes, A leap of faith,
To take you to your placing.
A Place of purpose… Your assignments.
Kingdom assignment.

Corinthians 12:9
My Grace towards you is such that my Glory will shine through you and my Power be seen upon you.

Do not look back.
Do not be weary of the past.
It is, what it Is.
Behold a new thing awaits before thee.
Sensitize yourself to the winds of change,
Refreshing wind blowing upon you.
A new awaits...
Refreshing wind cometh.

Isaiah 43:19
Behold, I will do a new thing now it shall spring forth, shall ye not know it? I will even make a way in the wilderness and rivers in the desert.

A great awakening.
An awareness,
Can you discern it not?
It's here,
It's here,
The promise, fulfillment in time.
That awaiting promise,
Step into the Promise.

Acts 2:28
Thou hast made known to me the ways of life; thou shalt make me full of joy with thy countenance.

In his presence,
There is solace.
I bow down in awe of you Lord.
My Lord; My Lord.
Abba, Abba.

Psalm 139
Though knowest my down-sitting and mine uprising,
though
understandeth my thoughts afar off.

Do not be weary,
Do not freight, he is there watching over you.
Call upon him you do…
Surrender!
In thy total surrender, for you shall find comfort and peace.
In his presence, there is no other…
There cannot be any other like him.
For he is the Lord of Hosts; marvelous you are Lord.

Psalm 91:4
He shall cover thee with his feathers and under his wings shalt though trust: his truth shall be thy shield and buckler.

Love, Peace, Happiness.
Let it flow, flow,
In perfect harmony.
Let it flow…let it flow.
For in thy presence I shall dwell.
Let it flow let it flow,
In perfect harmony, with thy Lord.

Psalm 113:7
He raiseth up the poor out of the dust and lifteth the needy
out of the dung-hill.

Your purpose,
Your purpose,
Your fullness revealed.
Deep within you,
It's there, it's there.
With a time, it will be revealed.

Ephesians 3:7
But unto every one of us is given grace, according to the measure of the gift of Christ.

Be still.
Be comforted and remain steadfast,
For deep within thy soul,
Treasures abound…
Awaiting… Awaiting…

Isaiah 45:3
And I will give thee the treasures of darkness, and hidden riches of secret places, that thou mayest know that I, the LORD, which call thee by thy name am the GOD of Israel.

Adonai! Adonai! Adonai!
In whom I trust.
Resting in you Lord,
Pouring out my burdens, unto you.
He answers…! My Yoke is broken…
Free… I am free…
Trusting and knowing, knowingly all is well.

Isaiah 40:31
But they that wait upon the LORD shall renew their strength; they shall mount up the wings as eagles, they shall run, and not be weary; and they shall walk, and not faint.

In thy stillness,
The calmness to be.
At peace you shall be,
Happiness shall abound to thee...

Ephesians 2:10
For we are his workmanship, created in Christ Jesus unto good works, which God hath before ordained that we should walk in them.

Who are you?
For you know who you are,
And that you are.
Fulfillment in all that is to be,
In alignment, that is to be so.
Perfected harmony overall.

1 Peter 5:10–11
But the God of grace, who hath called us unto his eternal glory by Christ Jesus, after that ye have suffered a while make you perfect, stablish, strengthen, settle you. To him be glory and dominion forever and ever, Amen.

Lead me as you so will,
Chastise me as you so will.
For at the end of it all,
The light…
The light shineth abundantly upon me.

Philippians 4:13
I can do all things through Christ which strengthened me.

Evoke within me,
A greater awakening.
To be, that I am to be.
Fulfillment of who I am ought to be.
My source of strength, so he is.
Mighty, you are ABBA.

2 Peter 1:11
For so an entrance shall be ministered unto you abundantly
into the everlasting
Kingdom of our LORD and savior Jesus Christ.

We cry,
We laugh,
All hope is not lost.
All hope from him we seek,
All that we hope for shall be.

Job 8:21
Till he fills thy mouth with laughing and thy lips with rejoicing.

Faith, faith,
A word or deed?
Faith, faith
Deep within thy soul.
Oh! Faith; Oh Faith,
Are you a he or she?
Let Grace of Faith abound to me.

Hebrew 10:23
Let us hold fast the profession of our faith without waver-
ing; for he is faithful that promised.

Glory to thee,
You are mighty.
Glory to thee,
In thy majesty.
You reign, you reign.
Watching over us, yes you do.

Philippians 4:19
But my God shall supply all your needs according to his riches in glory by Christ Jesus.

Tears, tears yes they are.
Tears, tears,
He wipes them away.
A promise that is to be so,
Comforted you shall be.
For thy tears, shall be apart from thee.
Thy sorrow shall depart from thee.

Psalm 34:17
The righteous cry, and the LORD *heareth, and delivereth them out of their*
troubles.

Arise, Arise,
With boldness, you stand.
Arise, arise…!
Your portion awaits for thee…

1 Peter 3:12
For the eyes of the Lord are over the righteous, and his ears
are open unto their prayers: but the face

Laughter, laughter,
Aloud it is.
Happiness, joyfulness outpours from deep within.
If you pursue and uphold it,
It will abide to thee.

Colossians 1:11
Strengthened with all might, according to his glorious power, unto all patience and long-suffering with joyfulness.

Victory!
Oh, victorious I am.
For whatsoever comes my way,
Focused I will be.
Victory, victory,
So, it is.

2 Corinthians 2:14
Now thanks be unto God, which always causeth us to triumph in Christ, and maketh manifest the savor of his knowledge by us in every place.

Dance, Dance.
Be merry, be of good cheer.
Laughter will ignite a relief…
As you laugh,
All that is withholding,
Shall be released.

Romans 8:28
And we all know that all things work together for good to them that love God, to them who are called according to his purpose.

Thy walk,
Our walk of life,
Narrow are thy paths.
Thy walk, our walk, as we journey.
Winding, narrow roads…
Rocky, paths they might be.
Deep in the valley,
Ascending to the mountain top…
Clear horizons they shall be.

Psalm 25:4
Show me thy ways; O Lord; teach me thy paths.

You are gracious,
Gracious you are.
Thankful for that's to come as I seek.
Ever so grateful for that shall be.
Yes I am.

Luke 11:10
For everyone that asketh receiveth, and he that seeketh fin-
deth and to him that knocketh it shall be opened unto you.

I know where I have been,
I know where I am coming from.
I leap, I jump, I sing.
For I know where I am at,
Yes, I do know where I am ought to be…
I am getting there,
Yes I am.

Psalm 136:1
Give thanks unto the Lord, *for he is good; for his mercy endureth forever.*

Who are you in him?
Do you know who you are?
Yes, a conduit that I am,
Perceive it not to be so...
A vessel that I am, for the Master's use.
Let no man put asunder,
For that's who I am.
For I know who I am.

John 15:16
Ye have not chosen me, but I have chosen you and ordained
you that ye should go and bring forth fruit, and that fruit
should remain, that whatsoever ye shall ask of the Father in
my name, he may give it to you.

In thy fullness of you Lord,
In thy presence.
Only then shall I find myself, immersed in thy goodness.
Thy fullness of you Adonai,
A glimpse, of thy gracious power imparted upon me.
The love of thy Lord.

Isaiah 41:10
Fear thou not; for I am with thee: be not dismayed, for I am thy GOD: I will strengthen thee yea, I will help thee; yea, I will uphold thee with the right hand of my righteousness.

You are ever so faithful Lord.
A fulfillment of thy promises,
As they unfold before me…
In thy presence…only then shall I find.
Thy gracious power and grace,
Imparted upon me to become what is to be.
The love of our Lord God.

Ephesians 2:8
For by grace are you saved through faith, and that not of
yourself it is the gift of God.

Can you see it?
Shall you not see it?
For it is there.
Treasures they are,
Waiting, for those that are to receive.

Isaiah 45:3
And I will give thee treasures of darkness, and hidden riches
of secret places that though mayest know that I, the LORD
which call you by name am the God of Israel.

Here I am,
For I can attest.
for the past is the past.
Foresight and focus,
for that's to be.
Strengthened I am, for it to become so.
For I see…
Rejoicing and Joyfulness shall be.

1 Corinthians 15:10
But by the grace of God I am that I am, what I am: and his grace which was bestowed upon me was not in vain: I labored more abundantly than they all, yet not, I but the grace of God which was with me.

In despair you might be,
There is one that you ought to seek.
Strengthened you shall be,
For faithful he is.
Yes, he is,
Adonai.

Ephesians 2:8
For by grace are you saved through faith: and that not of
yourselves

To you we look up to,
Fail us not Lord.
Trusting in you with all,
Yes, my all.
Fail me not I plead with thee, Lord.
Fail me not, I plead with thee.

Psalm 92:11
For he shall give his angels charge over thee, to keep thee in all thy ways.

Thankful Lord, I give you all my praise;
I give unto you, glorious praise.
Thirsty that I am, as I seek deeper in what you have for
me LORD.
Thirsting for more, so true it is...
I am receptive of thy grace as I can be.
Oh, yes Lord,
Settled at peace I shall be.

John 1:16
And of his fullness have all we received and Grace for Grace.

OH, greater!
You are Creator, the King of kings,
You reign on High,
Oh, high…higher, higher…!
Looking upon his creations…
Creator marvels…
The great mighty power he beholds.
Our Creator he is.

Genesis 1:31
And God saw everything that he had made, and behold, it
was very good. And the evening and the morning.

Hope!
For we all hope.
Yes, we do.
With the faith that from within,
We shall find solace, for that we hope for.
Anchored to that we wish to become so.

Isaiah 40:31
*But they that wait upon the L*ORD *shall renew their strength,*
they shall run, and not be weary; and they shall walk and
not faint.

Hebrew 11:1
Now faith is the substance of things hoped for; the evidence
of things not seen.

More and more.
Do we not yearn for all that is so hoped for…?
Greater magnitude of goodness, all that to unveil before
us.
At peace, we will be.
With thanksgiving upon thy lips,
Grateful as can be.

2 Corinthians 9:8
For God is able to make all grace abound towards you, that ye, always having all sufficiency in all things may abound to every good work.

Deeper and deeper in love with him.
For that's where it is;
The essence of greatness.
For the unseen…
With boldness forever behold…
Deeper and Deeper…
Take hold tightly, all that you receive.

Psalm 65:13
The pastures are clothed with flocks; the valleys also are covered over with corn: they shout for joy, they also sing.

Forever I shall be.
Gratefulness and gratitude, flowing from deep within
thee.
Overwhelming,
Overflow...
Inexpressible it might be.
Thy glowing face shall reveal it all.

Psalm 119:18
*Open though mine eyes, that I may behold the wondrous
things out of thy law.*

The fullness in all to be;
Let thy fullness that I ought to…become so.
That which I was created to be.
Let me become that is to be so.
Fulfillment it will be, as he so wills.

Psalm 21:6
For Thou hast made him most blessed forever: thou hast made him exceedingly
glad about thy countenance.

Awaiting in anticipation, my expectations…
For we all have.
Will they be fulfilled…?
At that moment, merry thy shall be.

Psalm 25:6
Remember, oh LORD, *thy tender mercies and thy loving*
kindness for they are
have been ever of old.

Ignorance and Wisdom;
Should there really be a comparison?
Ignorance; self-centeredness with pride.
Certainly, you shall be blinded and stumble…
Wisdom; let you be mindful and sensitive to words of speech and deeds…
Elevation shall be thy portion.

Ephesians 4:32
And be kind to one another, tenderhearted, forgiving one another even as God for Christ's sake hath forgiven you.

Yes, I can see.
Not with thy eyes that you have…
Yes, I can see… Spiritual sight it is.
Discernment as I perceive,
Thy sight, a gift it is.
Yes, I can see.
Revelation, with boldness unfolds…

Isaiah 61:1
The spirit of the Lord GOD is upon me; because the LORD hath anointed me to preach good tidings unto the meek, he hath sent me to bind up the broken hearted, to proclaim liberty to the captives, and the opening of the prison to them that are bound.

Here we are.
For we know not…
That in which the future beholds.
Ought we to look up to him?
As we rest, in the warmth of his presence.
As you smile upon me Lord,
Consolation…the safest place to be.

Psalm 91:4
He shall cover thee with his feathers and under the wings,
shalt though trust. His truth shall be thy shield and buckler.

Eyes gazing…
His Eyes gazing.
The Lord thy God will never abandon you.
Neither shall he forsake you.
He is there…
He is here…
Watching over you he is.
Shall you seek him?
Do so!
Faithful and kindness
Forevermore.

Psalm 31:5
Into thine hand I commit my spirit: though hast redeemed me, O LORD GOD of truth.

Your faithfulness,
Your gentleness…
Your touch…embraced in thy warmness.
Your smile upon me ABBA.

John 4:24
God is a spirit and they that worship him must worship him in spirit and in truth.

I know where I have been…
I know, where I am coming from.
I leap, I jump, I sing…
I know, where I am at.
For I know, where I ought to be.
For he is faithful, yes he is,
So true to his promises…
Yes, I am getting there, yes I am.

Psalm 31:3
For thou art my rock and my fortress; therefore for thy name's sake lead me and guide me.

For I don't know for certain,
That is, or is to be.
Uncertainty beholds the darkness…
Destruction, obscured by thy thoughts…
The foundation of what is to become, shall not be lost.
Positivity is all that we ought to be.

Jeremiah 29:11
For I know the thoughts that I think towards you: saith
the LORD, thoughts of peace, and not of evil, to give you an
expected end.

For those who are called to release a divine word;
Healing, deliverance, that is to be so.
As to why?
Selective they are…
A fulfillment word in season, they select…
Not to be so…!
Cautious you ought to be.
For envious they are, for that is to be…

Isaiah 41:10
Fear though not, for I am with thee be not be dismayed; for I am thy God: I will strengthen thee, yea, I will help thee, yes I will uphold thee with the right hand of my righteousness.

Thankful, I am,
Grateful as I can be.
All hope that's becoming,
No lost cause.
For there is only that I hope for…
The unseen that yields fruition.
Yes, thankful as I am,
Joyous as I can be.

Amos 3:7
Surely the LORD GOD will do nothing, but he revealeth his
secret unto his servant prophet.

Awaiting…
For all those that await;
Waiting for that promise.
Promise of truth which is to become so.
Despair not!
For it's in his promise,
Yes, that promise…that's becoming.
Yes, yes, fulfillment in time.
It shall be!

Isaiah 55:11
So shall my word be that goeth forth out of my mouth: it
shall not return
unto me void, but it shall accomplish that which I please,
and it shall
prosper in the thing where to I send it.

For if he is the one,
Let all that he does reveal in word and deed…
Happiness and fulfillment unveiled.
Let it be seen, for him to be the gift that he is.
Ordained by you; Lord Adonai.
Placed upon my bosom, the love I long waited for…

Ephesians 5:28
So, ought men to love their wives as their own bodies. He who loveth his wife loveth himself.

Wind of fresh;
Blow, blow
Swiftly upon me…
In thy presence,
Refreshing it is.
Impartation for that is becoming,
Shaken I tremble.
Blow, blow,
Divine breath upon me.
Grasp tightly, to what is to be so…

Isaiah 66:2
For all those things hath mine hand made and all those things have been, saith the LORD, *but to this man will I look, even to him that is poor and of a contrite spirit, and trembleth at my word.*

I sing, I sing, yes I sing!
Words of hope,
Words that heal.
Deliverance that is to come;
Open thy eyes, awareness to signs, for you shall see.
Transformation and manifestation in great, glorious
splendor.

Psalm 111:3–5
*The works of the Lord are great, sought out all them that
have pleasure therein. His work is honorable and glorious
and his righteousness endureth forever. He hath made his
wonderful works to be remembered: the Lord is glorious
and full of compassion.*

A cry out;
Open heavens abound to thee!
Overwhelmed you shall be.
Gratefulness and gratitude.
Grace to synchronize, all that is before thee.
Open heavens!
Blessings upon blessings, upon thee.
Yes, thy eyes shall see.

2 Kings 25:30
And his allowance was a continual allowance given to him of the king, a daily rate for every day, all the days of his life.

Your faithfulness.
Your gentleness, your touch!
As I await unto the birth of the new,
For you smiling upon me Lord.
Fresh wind; blowing gently upon me.
Wind of fresh. Yes, it is!
Your touch, your love,
The warmth of thy embrace Elohim.

Matthew 11:9
But what went you out to see? A prophet? Yea, I say unto
you, and more than a prophet.

All that is springing forth,
All that is becoming.
Morning mildew, nourishing that is to be.
Springing forth.
Oh, it's becoming...
Forcefully it springs forth.
Tenderness thy new, in its glorious splendor!
Nurture it for it's delicately so.
Loving it, for yours it is.
Springing forth.
For it sprang forth with tenderness.

1 Peter 5
Casting all your care upon him, for he careth for you.

Grace, grace.
For what is grace?
Sacred it is.
Chosen few to receive, receptive they should be.
Grace, grace.
The essence of all things to be.
Patience is the essence for manifestation of all that is to become so.
In thy essence of all that is.
Tallying and abandonment to the things that are to be.
Lost time, sadly you shall miss it all.
Grace, grace, for sacred it is.

Romans 11:5
Even so then at this present time also there is a remnant according to the election of grace.

Walk in the light!
In the light for you to be.
Only in the light,
For you to see.
Only in the light, were there is greatness.
Brightness abounds.
Only in the light, at peace you shall be.
All darkness dispelled...
For all the unseen, revealed and fled.
Only in the light, for us to see clearly.
Happiness and peace unfold...
Only in the light, where I belong in his comfort.
Only in the light, where I ought to be.

Psalm 73:24–25
Though shall guide me with thy counsel, and afterwards receive me to glory. Who have I in heaven but thee? And there is none upon earth that I desire but thee.

In silence, swiftly it blows upon you.
Be still in thy presence.
Only in thy stillness.
Soft whispers shall you hear.
Attentively thereon you shall perceive
Only in thy stillness for you to hear his voice.
Yes he speaks!
Be still, Be still.
In thy silence you shall hear him.

John 4:14
But whosoever drinketh of the water that I shall give him
shall never thirst, but the water that I shall give him shall
be in him a well of water springing up into everlasting life.

Do we all not have a purpose?
A journey that we embark.
Down the valley, up thy hills…
Need we all strength to pursue to all that is to be
Yes, thy paths led to thy destiny.
Holding onto the promise.

1 Colossians 2:7
Rooted and built up in him, and established in faith, as you have been taught, abounding therein in thanksgiving.

Who am I Lord?
For can I express, what is best for me Lord.
Only you can make it to be.
Only you, for it's you, that know what is best for me.

1 Corinthians 3:7
So, neither is he that planteth anything. Neither he that watereth are one.
And every man shall receive his own reward according to his own labor.
For we are laborers of God; ye are.
God's husbandry you are.
God's building.

New dawn, new day.
As we step in anticipation,
Of the new…
Let it be, that is to be.
Let the rays of sunshine shine.
Let it shine brightly.

Psalm 30:5
Weeping may endure for the night but joy comes in the morning.

A fulfillment, of what I am ought to be.
Fulfillment, of who I am.
All that is to be, to that is vast before me…
A fulfillment, yes, a fulfillment…
Positioned to the placement that I am ought to be.

Colossians 1:12
Giving thanks unto the father, which hath made us need to be partakers of the inheritance of the Saints in light.

For you know not, all that is to become so.
Beholding in deep essence, of what is, and to be...
For all that is to be our eyes shall behold.
All that ought to be, for all to see,
Shall be...

Ephesians 1:18
The eye of your understanding being enlightened, that ye
may know what is the hope of his calling, and what the
riches of the glory of his inheritance in the Saints.

What is it that you hope for?
Clinging…unto your inner knowing.
Yearning for that which is not.
Perseverance, against all odds.
Only with thy hope, and thy resilience,
Thou shall be, were you ought to be.
Hope, hope, hope…
Faithfully and hopeful…

Psalm 31:3
For thou art my rock and my fortress; therefore for thy name's sake lead me, and guide me.

Here I am,
As I so will.
Take over, as you so will.
Taken as you control
I in total surrender.
For all to become so.
At the Master's feet I shall be,
Close proximity for I to receive.
Blessings, abound to me,
Wisdom so to speak.
Knowledgeable to the sacred,
Yes, for a chosen few to perceive.
Blessings abound to me…

Ephesians 3:20
Now unto him that is able to do exceedingly, abundantly
above all that we ask or think, according to the power that
worketh in us.

Give me the Grace to do the right thing by you,
As you will Lord.
Give me the Grace to do that which is pleasing in thy
sight,
Amen.
In the know,
Thoughts afar…
Deeply, yes you're searching.
In the know,
What is it you treasure most?
So deep that's within,
Nestled in thy depthness.
In the know,
For you know what you know.
Sealed so deep within.
So deep within it is secured in depthness.

Numbers 6:24–25
The Lord bless thee and keep thee. The Lord make his face
shine upon thee and be gracious unto thee.

Light, light,
Let there be light.
Shine, shining upon us.
Rays of light, rest upon us,
Arrays of…yes arrays, that glow…
In thy brightness, it shines upon me,
Yes, for that's the dwelling place you ought to be.
Shine, shining brightly.

Psalm 71:23
My lips shall greatly rejoice when I sing unto thee and my soul which though hast redeemed.

Wind of fresh…
Blow, blow,
Swiftly upon me…
His glory in thy presence.
Refreshing it is!
Impartation, for that's becoming,
Shaken, you tremble.
Grasp tightly to what is to be so…
Blow, blow,
Divine breath upon me.

John 15:7
If ye abide in me, and my words abide in you, you shall ask
what you will and it shall be done unto you.

To do or not to…
For what is to do?
For you know not, how to!
All that is to be,
Only if you do, that needed to be.
That's to be, shall be.
That which is not to be.
Shall not be done so.
For thou shall not do.
To do or not to?

Revelation 22:12
And, behold, I come quickly; and my reward is with me, to give every man according as his works, shall be.

Be aligned to all that is,
For all that's to become so.
For it's only you who can,
Perceive so.
Only with you for it to be.

Psalm 18
The Lord is my rock and my fortress and my deliverer; my
God, my strength in whom I will trust, my buckler and the
horn of my salvation and my high tower.

Say, say what?
All that's to be said.
So Deep within.
All that's resurfacing…
Say, Say for I ought to.
Silence broken!
All that's to be spoken,
With quivering lips, I say?
Uncertainty, for how it's to be perceived.
Silence, not to withstand,
For with boldness, I stand.

Psalm 18:6
In my distress, I call upon thee Lord and cried unto my G OD *he heard my voice out of his temple and my cry came before him, even into his ears.*

For all that is to be.
As you will.
For where I am at?
As you so will.
Let thy light, shine brightly,
Shine, shine brightly.
So you will,
For all that is yet, to spring forth.
Your will, as you so will.

Psalm 111:6
He has shown his people the power of his works, that he
may give them the heritage of the heathen.

Let it flow,
Let it flow, flow...
Flow, flowing harmoniously.
Let it flow...
Flow, flow in synchronicity.
Let it flow...
Flowing!
Let it Flow expeditiously,
Flow, flow, it's flowing...

Ephesians 4:7
But unto every one of us is given grace, according to the measure of the gift of Christ.

Love and cherish me for all that I am.
All that I am.
For all the flaws you foresee.
Swept away you are, not to see.
Cherish all moments to be.
All that is, for it is who I am.
With tenderness, your eyes behold.
For you see within me,
All that you behold
Anticipation for all that's to become so.

Songs of Solomon 8:2
Many waters cannot quench love, neither can the floods drown it: if a man would give all the substance of his house for love it would utterly be contemned.

Thy grace which is upon you,
For that which is so.
Sustenance of that which you have received,
The source of all that's becoming…
Ought you not to forget, lift thy eye up.
Thy face enlightened with happiness and gratitude.
A whisper,
"Thank you creator…"
ABBA my Father.

Deuteronomy 16:17
Every man shall give as is able, according to the blessings of
the LORD thy God which he hath given thee.

Special you,
There is only that special you.
Slipped away unexpectedly.
Turned to dust for us not to see.
Special you are...
Ever so kind, yes you were.
Your child/children so young,
All the unforeseen time that you lost.
Be at peace...
Yes, tears we shed.
For special you are,
Ever so kind you were.
Memories of you we uphold, for we know you cared.

Psalm 34:18
The Lord is near to the brokenhearted and saves the crushed in spirit.

Psalm 73:26
My flesh and my heart faileth: but God is the strength of my heart, and my portion forever.

For is, there is.
With that we have.
Anticipating for what is not,
For all that is.
Is it?
For it's not what is to be,
So deeply you're searching.
Only then, shall you find that is.
For you have been given.
Clenched it was in thy fists.
Only then, when you realize who you are.
For if not,
You shall travail.
Let not you be weary,
Be persistent.
For there it is, awaiting.
Open thy eyes to see,
Oooh, how you shall marvel.
For it's only that you have,
Let it not be lost.

2 Peter 1:2–3
Grace and peace be multiplied unto you through the knowledge of God, and of Jesus our Lord, according as his divine power hath given unto us all things that pertain unto life and godliness, through the knowledge of him that hath called us to glory and virtue.

Looking,
Searching for that which is not,
For it's not.
So shall you ask, is it to be?
That you so deeply yearn for?
Oooh, it's not that you yet have,
As you visualize so earnestly.
Let it be,
That is to be.
With ease for you to see.
Yes, let that is of yours.
Be unto you to receive.

Ezekiel 37:14
And I shall put my spirit in you, and you shall live, and I shall place you in your own land then shall you know that I the Lord have spoken it and performed it saith the Lord.

Simply believe,
Believing, in that which is not.
For that I say, supernaturally…
Simply, believe!
Propelled to all that is to be.
We all, ought to say…
Simply believe!
All that's heard and learned…
Promises, that are to become so.
Yes, springing forth…

Psalm 59:17
Unto thee, O my strength, will l sing : for God is my defense
and the God of my mercy.

Blessed be thou, Lord God of Israel our father, forever and ever.

Thine OH LORD, is the greatness, and the power and the glory, and the victory, and the majesty: for all that is in the heaven and in the earth is thine; thine is the kingdom, O LORD, and thou art exalted as head above all. (1 Chronicles 29:10–11)

A megablessing, how can you be expectant of it? Yes, with continuous prayer, yet you're continually resistant to step out of your comfort zone. Take heed. It is delaying your answered prayers. *Step out*, and align yourself strategically to your heart's desire.

Both riches and honor come of thee, and though reigns over all; and in thine hand is power and might and in thine hand is to make great, and to give strength unto all.

Now therefore, our God, we thank thee, and praise thy *glorious name*. (1 Chronicles 29:12–13)

Amen.

Blessings and peace I speak forth, good health. A fulfillment to all that is to be so.

Blessings to you all for all years to be!

Ingram Content Group UK Ltd.
Milton Keynes UK
UKHW042002200623
423745UK00001B/58